DAVID PITHERS & SARAH GREENE

We Can Say
NO!

Illustrated by Kate Rogers

Published in association with
National Children's Home

BEAVER BOOKS

To Jane, James and David
with love and respect

A Beaver Book
Published by Arrow Books Limited
62–65 Chandos Place, London WC2N 4NW

An imprint of Century Hutchinson Ltd

London Melbourne Auckland Johannesburg
and agencies throughout the world

First published in 1986
Reprinted 1986 (Twice) and 1987

Set in 14pt Helvetica

Designed by Philippa Bramson

Printed and bound in Great Britain by Scotprint, Edinburgh

ISBN 0 09 950690 4

Notes for Adults

This is a book which should be used by adults and children together. The incidents it recounts are fictional and children will need help in understanding the general principles. The book's main purpose is to promote discussion between children and adults. Of course this will involve attention to the child's feelings – and here it is important to emphasize how strong and assertive a child can be. The situations described will be much less frightening if children feel that they can be powerful. Potential abductors operate under enormous stress, and when they are resisted they tend to get away as quickly as they can. That is why an immediate, assertive, 'No!' can usually stop inappropriate advances.

The point to emphasize is that your children should not keep secrets. This means that they must be convinced that you will believe them, that you will listen attentively, and that they will not be punished for what they have told you.

So, if you are confident with your children and confident in them they will be better equipped to deal with an experience we all hope they will never have to face.

David Pithers
Sarah Greene

Joanne is four.

She is very sure of herself. She likes her brother Tom but thinks he bosses her around too much, just because he is older.

But she loves his jokes.

Tom is seven.

He doesn't always want to do what he's told, and sometimes he gets into trouble.

Tom is very fond of his sister Joanne. After all, she laughs at his jokes.

Joanne and Tom know some very important things.

They know about road safety.

They know about fire and accidents.

They know about dangerous people.

These are people who may try to take
them away and hurt them.

But Joanne and Tom are

STRONG   CLEVER   CAREFUL   SAFE

Because they know when to say 'NO!'

You can be strong, clever, careful and safe too.

Joanne and Tom will show you how.

Most grown-ups are not dangerous.
But there are some who are.

They do not look like monsters.

They look like ordinary people.

Which grown-ups should you be careful of?

You must look out for what they say and do!

Tom and Joanne know that dangerous
people are very clever, but Tom
and Joanne are clever too.

Every year Tom and Joanne go on holiday with Mum. They stay in a guest house just across the road from the beach.

One day when they were on the beach Joanne wandered off on her own.

She was paddling in the sea when she dropped her bucket. A man ran into the sea and fetched it for her. Joanne had seen him before; he was staying in the same guest house. He seemed kind and he asked Joanne if she would like him to take her to buy an ice cream. Joanne loves ice cream.

She nearly went. But then she remembered what Mum had told her.

IT COULD BE A TRICK!

The man might want to take her away and make her do things she didn't want to do.

Joanne said '**NO!**'

She started to walk away quickly, without looking back.

The man came after her and tried to grab her arm.

Joanne kicked the man on the leg. She shouted,
'I DON'T KNOW HIM!' as loudly as she could, just as
Mum had told her.

The man didn't like Joanne shouting. He ran away.

A man and a woman heard Joanne. The man ran to fetch
the police. The woman waited with Joanne.

A policewoman came to talk to Joanne. Joanne knew she must not keep secrets. She told her everything that had happened.

The policewoman told Joanne that she had been very clever. She had done the right thing.

Afterwards, they all had ice creams. Tom thought Joanne was getting too much fuss. But he was also a bit proud of her. So was Mum!

BE STRONG CODE

If someone you don't know very well offers you a treat,

Say 'NO!'

IT COULD BE A TRICK!

If someone tries to touch you, kick them and shout as loud as you can,

'I DON'T KNOW HIM!'

Walk away quickly.

Do not run.

Do not look back.

Do not keep secrets.

Tell Mum or Dad what has happened. If Mum or Dad are not nearby, ask the nearest group of people to get the police.

Mr Lawrence lives in the flat below Tom and Joanne. Sometimes they pass him on the stairs and pat his dog.

One day Tom and Joanne were walking up the stairs when Mr Lawrence opened the door of his flat. He asked them if they would like to come in for orange squash and chocolate biscuits.

They nearly went.

Tom said he would ask Mum. But Mr Lawrence said Mum might not like it so they should not tell her. He said it would be their secret.

Tom felt a warning inside him.

IT COULD BE A TRICK!

Joanne wanted to go, but Tom said 'NO!' He took her hand and rushed her upstairs. When they got to their flat, Joanne sulked and would not talk to him.

But Tom knew that Mr Lawrence should have asked Mum first. He might want to hurt them or make them do things they didn't want to do.

When Tom told Mum what had happened she was very pleased with him.

Mum went to see Mr Lawrence and told him that he must not ask the children into his flat again. Mr Lawrence understood and seemed pleased that Mum had explained things to him.

Tom thought Joanne hadn't been so clever that time. But he didn't say so. Anyway, she was talking to him again . . . .

BE CLEVER CODE

If someone asks you into their flat or house,
say you have to ask Mum or Dad first.

If they ask you not to tell Mum or Dad,

Say 'NO!'

If they say they have already asked Mum or Dad,

Say 'NO!' and go to check.

IT COULD BE A TRICK!

If you are not sure

Say 'NO!'

One day Tom was waiting outside school for Mum and Joanne to collect him. He was tired and hungry and he wanted his tea.

Just as he was getting really cross, a man and a woman came along.

The woman said, 'Hello, Tom.' Tom was surprised that she knew his name as he had never seen her before. She seemed friendly though. 'I'm afraid Joanne is ill,' she said. 'Mum has sent us to fetch you.'

The teacher, Mrs Jones, took Tom to the staff room. Just at that moment, Mum came running up with Joanne. She said she was sorry she was late, she had missed the bus.

The man walked down the road to his car and opened the door.

But Tom felt that warning again.

IT COULD BE A TRICK!

He said 'NO!'

He turned round and walked straight back into school. He found a teacher and told her what had happened.

Tom and Mrs Jones told Mum what had happened. Mum and Mrs Jones went to see if the people were still there while another teacher phoned the police.

The people had gone, but Tom was able to tell the policeman what they looked like and the colour of the car. The policeman told Tom he would make a good detective.

Later that night when Mum was tucking Tom up in bed, he began to feel frightened. 'I nearly went with them,' he said, just managing not to cry.

Mum gave him a big hug and told him how glad she was that he had not. Then he cried a lot.

Joanne was quiet, but she was pleased she had an older brother who could still cry.

BE CAREFUL CODE

If someone other than Mum or the person who usually collects you arrives to take you home from school,

Say 'NO!'

Never get into anyone's car without Mum and Dad knowing.

IT COULD BE A TRICK!

Walk back into school quickly, without looking back.

Tell a teacher straight away.

If you are not sure,

Say 'NO!'

(Note for parents: never have your child's name on the outside of his or her clothing or belongings.)

One Saturday Tom and Joanne went shopping with Mum. The supermarket was very crowded and noisy. Joanne had some money of her own and she stopped to look at the sweets. She thought she would buy some for Tom too. After she had picked what she wanted she could not see Mum or Tom.

A man said 'Hello' to Joanne and asked if she would like some more sweets.

Joanne said '**NO!**'

IT COULD BE A TRICK!

Mum had told her what to do if she got lost.

She knew she must not leave the shop. She looked for the lady who takes the money at the till. Joanne said, 'I've lost my Mum.'

The lady looked after Joanne and asked the manager to call Mum on the loudspeaker.

A message came over the loudspeaker

WE HAVE A LITTLE GIRL CALLED JOANNE WHO HAS LOST HER MUM. SHE IS WAITING AT THE TILL.

Joanne liked to hear her name on the loudspeaker.

Mum came straight away. She was very pleased with Joanne. She had done the right thing. The lady at the till gave Joanne some sweets. Tom got some too.

BE SAFE CODE

If someone offers to buy you a treat.

Say 'NO!'

IT COULD BE A TRICK!

If you lose Mum and Dad when out shopping,
don't leave the shop.

Look for the lady who takes the money at the till.

Tell her you are lost and ask her to get the manager.

Tom and Joanne would also like to tell you about all the grown-ups they know who are not dangerous.

There's Louise, the babysitter who comes to look after them when Mum and Dad go out.

There's Uncle George and Auntie Claire who sometimes bring presents when they visit.

There's Mum and Dad's friend Paul, who sometimes takes them out for a treat.

There's Linda, who lives in the flat opposite, who sometimes invites them to tea.

These are people that Mum and Dad know very well. If they are taking Tom and Joanne out they always tell Mum or Dad first, and they always let Mum or Dad know what time they will bring them home. They never ask Tom and Joanne to keep important secrets.

REMEMBER most grown-ups are not dangerous. Can you tell the ones who are?

This is the end of our stories about Joanne and Tom.

They have tried to show you how to be
STRONG   CLEVER   CAREFUL   SAFE

Can you remember what they have shown you?

SAY 'NO!' WITH TOM AND JOANNE

(Child and adult to speak alternate lines.)

If someone offers you a treat.
Say 'NO!'

If someone wants you to keep secrets:
Say 'NO!'

If someone asks you into their house:
Say 'NO!'

If someone offers to take you home from school:
Say 'NO!'

If you get lost and someone asks you to go with them:
Say 'NO!'

If someone tries to touch you:
Say 'NO!'

If someone offers you a lift:
Say 'NO!'

If someone says they'll buy you something:
Say 'NO!'

If you're not sure, don't say 'yes':
Say 'NO!'

BE STRONG!   BE CLEVER!   BE CAREFUL!   BE SAFE!